This book belongs to:

....

....

For Chloe and Ben, too grown up to hold
my hand now, but you will hold my heart forever – H. H.

For my Dad, thank you for holding my hand
and keeping me safe – D. H.

An Imprint of Sterling Publishing Co., Inc.
1166 Avenue of the Americas
New York, NY 10036

SANDY CREEK and the distinctive SANDY CREEK logo are registered trademarks of Barnes & Noble, Inc.

Text © 2014 by QEB Publishing, Inc.
Illustrations © 2014 by QEB Publishing, Inc.

ISBN 978-1-4351-5537-4

Manufactured in Guangdong, China
Lot #:
6 8 10 9 7
03/17

Editor: Alexandra Koken
Designer: Verity Clark

The Otter Who Loved to Hold Hands

Heidi *and* Daniel Howarth

Sandy Creek
NEW YORK

Every night, when they go to sleep, Otto's family
hold hands so they don't drift apart. And every morning,
when they wake up, they all let go again.

Except for little Otto. . .

Otto worried about swimming.
He worried about diving and he
worried about getting lost.

But most of all, he worried
about being alone.

Every morning, Mom said,
"Please let go, Otto. I can't do
anything with you holding
my hand!"

But Otto shook his head.
He didn't want to let go.

"I can't swim on my own!"
he squealed, clinging onto Mom.

He knew he would float—
but letting go was still scary.

What if he drifted
out to sea?

"You can do it," Mom said gently.
But Otto shook his head.
He didn't want to let go.

The other cubs enjoyed
playing, chasing, and splashing.

Otto wanted to join in,
but he just couldn't let
go of Mom and Dad.

"Go and play," said Dad. "I'll watch
you from here."

But Otto shook his head.
He didn't want to let go.
"I'm scared!" Otto cried.

"Don't let go!" Otto begged, as Mom
tried to open an oyster shell.

"I'm still right here," Mom sighed.
But Otto just had to hold on.

Mom and the shell bobbed and
rocked as Otto clung to her.

When Mom finally opened the oyster shell, Otto saw a beautiful shiny pearl gleaming inside it.

"It's amazing," Otto said.
"Ooh, look! There's an otter
inside, just like me!"

Otto reached out to the little otter in the pearl and before he knew it. . .

. . .he was holding the
beautiful pearl in both
his hands.

Otto saw a happy otter
floating all by himself...

...and realized
it was him!

"We're so proud of you!" Mom said.
"Well done, Otto!" Dad said.

"I let go!" Otto cried. "I'm floating
on my own and I'm fine!"

"Hooray! Come and play with us!"
called the other little otters.

So now, every day,
Otto **splashes**

and **swims**

and **plays**
with his friends.

He's a very **happy** little otter.

But he still looks forward to nighttime,
when he and his family hold hands as
they drift off to sleep.